Hairy Maclary and Zachary Quack

Lynley Dodd

ABC BOOKS

It was drowsily warm,
with dozens of bees
lazily buzzing
through flowers and trees.
Hairy Maclary decided to choose
a space in the shade
for his afternoon
snooze.
He dozily dreamed
as he lay on his back
when …

pittery pattery,
skittery scattery,
Z I P
round the corner
came
Zachary Quack

who wanted to frolic
and footle
and play
but …

Hairy Maclary
skedaddled
away.

Over the lawn
and asparagus bed
went Hairy Maclary
to hide in the shed.
He lurked in the shadows
all dusty and black
but …

pittery pattery,
skittery scattery,
Z I P
round the corner
came
Zachary Quack.

Out of the garden
and into the trees
jumped Hairy Maclary
with springs
in his knees.
He hid in the grass
at the side of the track
but …

pittery pattery,
skittery scattery,
Z I P
round the corner
came
Zachary Quack.

Down to the river
through willow and reed
raced Hairy Maclary
at double the speed.
Into the water
he flew with a
S M A C K
but ...

pittery pattery,
skittery scattery,
Z I P
round the corner
came
Zachary Quack,
who dizzily dived
in the craziest way,
whirling
and swirling
in showers of spray.

Hairy Maclary
was off in a flash,
a flurry of bubbles,
a dog paddle splash.
He swam to the side
and floundered about,
he tried
and he tried
but he C O U L D N ' T
climb out.
Scrabbling upwards
and slithering back …
when

pittery pattery,
skittery scattery,
Z I P
through the water
came
Zachary Quack,
who sped round a corner
and,
showing the way,
led Hairy Maclary
up, up
and away.

Then,
soggy and shivering,
back up the track
went Hairy Maclary
with
Zachary Quack.

It was drowsily warm,
with dozens of bees
lazily buzzing
through flowers
and trees.
Hairy Maclary
decided to choose
a place in the shade
for his afternoon
snooze.
He dozily dreamed
as he lay on his back …

tucked up together
with
Zachary Quack.

Published in 1999 in Australia by
ABC Books for the
AUSTRALIAN BROADCASTING CORPORATION
GPO Box 9994 Sydney NSW 2001

First published in 1999 by
Mallinson Rendel Publishers Limited,
Wellington, New Zealand.

National Library of Australia
Cataloguing-in-Publication data

Dodd, Lynley.
Hairy Maclary and Zachary Quack.

ISBN 0 7333 0838 4

1. Ducks - Juvenile fiction. 2. Dogs - Juvenile fiction.
I. Australian Broadcasting Corporation. II. Title.
(Series: Hairy Maclary).

NZ823.2

Typeset in New Zealand
Printed in Hong Kong